John Greenleaf Whittier, Frederick O. Prince

Bronze Group Commemorating Emancipation

A gift to the city of Boston from Hon. Moses Kimball. Dedicated December

6, 1879

John Greenleaf Whittier, Frederick O. Prince

Bronze Group Commemorating Emancipation
A gift to the city of Boston from Hon. Moses Kimball. Dedicated December 6, 1879

ISBN/EAN: 9783337093051

Printed in Europe, USA, Canada, Australia, Japan

Cover: Foto ©Andreas Hilbeck / pixelio.de

More available books at **www.hansebooks.com**

EMANCIPATION

A RACE SET FREE
AND THE COUNTRY AT PEACE
LINCOLN
RESTS FROM HIS LABORS

BRONZE GROUP

COMMEMORATING

EMANCIPATION.

A GIFT TO THE CITY OF BOSTON

FROM

HON. MOSES KIMBALL.

Dedicated December 6, 1879.

CITY DOCUMENT No. 126.

PRINTED BY ORDER OF THE CITY COUNCIL.

1879.

PRESS OF
ROCKWELL & CHURCHILL
BOSTON.

CITY OF BOSTON.

In Board of Aldermen, December 8, 1879.

Ordered, That the oration of His Honor the Mayor, delivered at the dedication of the Statue of Abraham Lincoln, representing Emancipation, together with the address by Alderman Breck, the poem by John G. Whittier, and such other documents as may be of interest, be printed as a city document, under the direction of the Superintendent of Printing; and that five hundred extra copies be printed.

Passed. Sent down for concurrence. December 11, came up concurred. Approved by the Mayor December 12, 1879.

A true copy.

Attest:

S. F. McCLEARY,
City Clerk.

PRELIMINARY PROCEEDINGS.

At a meeting of the Board of Aldermen, June 3, 1879, the following communication was received from the Mayor : —

MAYOR'S OFFICE, CITY HALL,
BOSTON, June 3, 1879.

To the Honorable the City Council : —

I herewith transmit a communication from Hon. Moses Kimball, for such action as may seem fit and proper.

FREDERICK O. PRINCE,

Mayor.

BOSTON, May 30, 1879.

His Honor F. O. Prince, Mayor of Boston : —

DEAR SIR, — Having engaged of Mr. Thomas Ball a cast in bronze of his colossal group, emblematical of Emancipation, the central figure of which is a representation of the late President Lincoln, I have the honor to present the same to the City of Boston, conditioned that I may place it upon the triangular lot at the junction of Columbus avenue, Park square, and Pleasant street, and that the city will cause the area to be suitably enclosed and annually cultivated with flowering plants and shrubs.

The group is to arrive some time in August next.

Respectfully yours, etc.,

MOSES KIMBALL.

On motion of Alderman Breck, the communication was referred to a joint special committee and the Mayor.

The chairman appointed Aldermen Charles H. B. Breck, Daniel D. Kelly, and Solomon B. Stebbins, on the committee.

The Common Council, June 5, concurred in the reference, and added to the committee Councilmen Henry W. Swift of Ward 9, Nathan Sawyer of Ward 18, Paul H. Kendricken of Ward 20, Oscar B. Mowry of Ward 11, and Benjamin F. Anthony of Ward 19.

The committee submitted the following report : —

IN BOARD OF ALDERMEN, June 16, 1879.

The Joint Special Committee, to whom was referred the communication from the Honorable Moses Kimball, presenting to the city a bronze group emblematical of Emancipation, having considered the subject, respectfully recommend the passage of the following preamble, resolve, and orders.

For the Committee,

CHARLES H. B. BRECK,
Chairman.

Whereas, A communication has been received from the Honorable Moses Kimball, in which he tenders to the City of Boston the gift of a colossal group in bronze, emblematical of Emancipation, upon conditions that it be placed upon the lot of land at the junction of Columbus avenue, Park square, and Pleasant street, and that the city will cause the area to be suitably enclosed and annually cultivated with flowering plants and shrubs ; it is, therefore, hereby

Resolved, That the thanks of the City Council, in behalf of the citizens of Boston, be conveyed to the Honorable

Moses Kimball, for the public spirit displayed in his costly and substantial gift to the city, which is hereby accepted upon the conditions attached to his offer.

Ordered, That the triangular lot of land situated at the junction of Columbus avenue, Park square, and Pleasant street be, and the same is hereby assigned for the location of said group.

Ordered, That the Committee on Common and Public Grounds be requested to take such action as may be necessary to cause the said lot to be put in order and enclosed with a suitable fence, in accordance with the terms of the gift.

The preamble, resolve, and orders were passed by the Board of Aldermen, and in concurrence, June 26, by the Common Council; June 28 they were approved by the Mayor.

August 4 Alderman Breck submitted the following to the Board of Aldermen : —

The Committee on Common and Public Grounds, who were requested to cause the lot of land at the junction of Columbus avenue, Park square, and Pleasant street to be put in order, and enclosed with a suitable fence, in accordance with the terms of the gift of the Honorable Moses Kimball of the group emblematical of Emancipation, would respectfully report as follows : The committee have conferred with the City Architect, and he has furnished a design for a suitable fence and curb to be erected upon the aforesaid lot, and an estimate of the cost of the same, including the fencing and grading, amounting to $4,500. The committee are of the opinion that the cost of the above can be paid from the income of the Phillips Street-Fund, so called.

They respectfully recommend the passage of the accompanying order.

For the Committee,

HUGH O'BRIEN,
Chairman.

Ordered, That the Committee on Common and Public Grounds on the part of the Board of Aldermen be authorized to put in suitable order the lot of land at the junction of Columbus avenue, Park square, and Pleasant street, on which is to be placed the group emblematical of Emancipation, the gift to the city of the Honorable Moses Kimball, and to erect a fence and curb around the same ; the cost, not exceeding $4,500, to be paid from the income of the Phillips Street-Fund.

The order was read twice and passed.

In the Common Council, September 25. 1879, Mr. Swift of Ward 9 offered an order : That the Committee of the Board of Aldermen on the Erection of the Statue of Josiah Quincy, and the Joint Special Committee in charge of the statue commemorating Emancipation, acting together, be authorized to make suitable arrangements for the dedication of both of said statues ; the expense attending the same, not exceeding one thousand dollars, to be charged to the appropriation for Incidentals.

The order was passed, and the Board of Aldermen, September 29, concurred.

The committee having charge of the Quincy Statue were His Honor the Mayor, and Aldermen Joseph A. Tucker, Solomon B. Stebbins, and Daniel D. Kelley.

DESCRIPTION OF THE MONUMENT.

This work was conceived and executed by Mr. Ball, under the first influence of the news of Mr. Lincoln's assassination.

The original group was in Italian marble, and differs in some respects from the bronze group. In the original the kneeling slave is represented as perfectly passive, receiving the boon of freedom from the hand of the great liberator. But the artist justly changed this, to bring the presentation nearer to the historical fact, by making the emancipated slave an agent in his own deliverance. He is accordingly represented as exerting his own strength, with strained muscles, in breaking the chain which had bound him. A greater degree of dignity and vigor, as well as of historical accuracy, is thus imparted. The original was also changed by introducing, instead of an ideal slave, the figure of a living man, — the last slave ever taken up in Missouri under the fugitive slave law, and who was rescued from his captors (who had transcended their legal authority) under the orders of the provost-marshal of St. Louis. His name was Archer Alexander, and his condition of servitude legally continued until emancipation was proclaimed and became the law of the land. A photographic picture was sent to Mr. Ball, who has given both the face and manly bearing of the negro. The ideal group is thus converted into the literal truth of history without losing anything of its artistic conception or effect.

The monument in Park square stands on a triangular plat

of ground in front of the Providence Railroad station. A well-laid curb and sidewalk of pressed brick surround the plat. Inside the sidewalk the foundation of the group is raised two and a half feet and surrounded by heavy granite containing-stones. Around this is a bronze railing. Within it is the group. Two steps, of Cape Ann granite, are at the base, upon which stands the heavy octagonal die that supports the group. This is a solid block of red polished granite from Jonesborough, Me., and weighs about sixteen tons. No inscription is on this die.

The figure of President Lincoln is standing by a monolith, upon which is a book, and in his hand, which is resting on the monolith, is a scroll, representing the proclamation. The left hand is extended over the crouching figure of the slave, seeming to bid him arise and be free.

On the inner side of the monolith is a raised shield, with the stars and stripes; at the angle nearest the spectator, looking toward the front, is a bundle of fasces, with a bound axe; on the next face is a medallion head of Washington, and at the bottom the words, "Thomas Ball, sc., 1874." At the base of the bronze in front of the statue, in heavy raised letters, is the word

EMANCIPATION.

On the front of the base, in heavy raised polished letters, are the words : —

A RACE SET FREE.

AND THE COUNTRY AT PEACE.

LINCOLN

RESTS FROM HIS LABORS.

On the back, in raised unpolished letters, is this inscription : —

GIVEN TO THE CITY OF BOSTON

BY MOSES KIMBALL,

1879.

At the corners of the base are four large bronze vases for flowers. They are of Greek design, twenty inches high and thirty-one in diameter.

At each angle of the triangular plat is to be placed a gas-light, composed of a cluster of three lights, making the group perfectly distinct during the night.

The height of the granite die is six feet two inches ; thickness, six feet eight inches ; height of group from top of die, nine feet six inches ; height of the whole above the sidewalk. twenty-four feet six inches.

The group was cast in Munich at the royal foundery.

THE PROCLAMATION

OF

EMANCIPATION.

By the President of the United States of America.

A PROCLAMATION.

WHEREAS, on the twenty-second day of September, in the year of our Lord one thousand eight hundred and sixty-two, a proclamation was issued by the President of the United States, containing among other things the following, to wit:

"That on the first day of January, in the year of our Lord one thousand eight hundred and sixty-three, all persons held as slaves within any State, or designated part of a State, the people whereof shall then be in rebellion against the United States, shall be then, thenceforth, and forever free, and the Executive Government of the United States, including the military and naval authorities thereof, will recognize and maintain the freedom of such persons, and will do no act or acts to repress such persons, or any of them, in any efforts they may make for their actual freedom.

"That the Executive will, on the first day of January aforesaid, by proclamation, designate the States and parts of States, if any, in which the people therein respectively shall then be in rebellion against the United States, and the fact that any State, or the people thereof, shall on that day be in

good faith represented in the Congress of the United States
by members chosen thereto, at elections wherein a majority
of the qualified voters of such States shall have participated,
shall, in the absence of strong countervailing testimony, be
deemed conclusive evidence that such State and the people
thereof are not then in rebellion against the United States."

Now, therefore, I, Abraham Lincoln, President of the
United States, by virtue of the power in me vested as Com-
mander-in-chief of the Army and Navy of the United States
in time of actual armed rebellion against the authority and
Government of the United States, and as a fit and necessary
war measure for suppressing said rebellion, do, on this first
day of January, in the year of our Lord one thousand eight
hundred and sixty-three, and in accordance with my purpose
so to do, publicly proclaimed for the full period of one
hundred days from the day of the first above-mentioned
order, designate, as the States and parts of States
wherein the people thereof respectively are this day in rebellion against the United States, the following, to wit:
Arkansas, Texas, Louisiana, except the parishes of St.
Bernard, Plaque Mines, Jefferson, St. John, St. Charles, St.
James, Ascension, Assumption, Terre Bonne, Lafourche, St.
Mary, St. Martin, and Orleans, including the City of New
Orleans, Mississippi, Alabama, Florida, Georgia, South
Carolina, North Carolina, and Virginia, except the forty-
eight counties designated as West Virginia, and also the
counties of Berkeley, Accomac, Northampton, Elizabeth
City, York, Princess Ann, and Norfolk, including the cities
of Norfolk and Portsmouth, and which excepted parts are,
for the present, left precisely as if this proclamation were not
issued.

And by virtue of the power and for the purpose aforesaid,
I do order and declare that all persons held as slaves within
said designated States and parts of States are and hencefor-

ward shall be free; and that the Executive Government of the United States, including the Military and Naval authorities thereof, will recognize and maintain the freedom of said persons.

And I hereby enjoin upon the people so declared to be free, to abstain from all violence, unless in necessary self-defence, and I recommend to them, that in all cases, when allowed, they labor faithfully for reasonable wages.

And I further declare and make known that such persons of suitable condition will be received into the armed service of the United States to garrison forts, positions, stations, and other places, and to man vessels of all sorts in said service.

And upon this, sincerely believed to be an act of justice, warranted by the Constitution, upon military necessity, I invoke the considerate judgment of mankind and the gracious favor of Almighty God.

In witness whereof, I have hereunto set my hand and caused the seal of the United States to be affixed.

[L. S.]   Done at the City of Washington, this first day of January, in the year of our Lord one thousand eight hundred and sixty-three, and of the Independence of the United States of America the eighty-seventh.

ABRAHAM LINCOLN.

By the President — WILLIAM H. SEWARD,
Secretary of State.

THE DEDICATION.

PROGRAMME.

AT PARK SQUARE.

Unveiling of the Group, by the City Architect, in presence of the Committee, at 12 o'clock.

AT FANEUIL HALL.

His Honor Mayor Prince presiding.

MUSIC . Brown's Brigade Band.

PRAYER By the Rev. Phillips Brooks.

POEM . . . . By John G. Whittier,

Read by Master Andrew Chamberlain, of the Boston Latin School.

MUSIC.

Presentation of the Group to the City of Boston, by Alderman Charles H. B. Breck, Chairman of the Committee.

ORATION,

By His Honor, Mayor Prince.

BENEDICTION.

MUSIC.

THE DEDICATION EXERCISES.

The exercises occurred in accordance with the preceding programme, in the presence of a crowded audience of ladies and gentlemen, seated in Faneuil Hall. The committee originally intended to have the dedicatory exercises in Park Square, around the group, but in consequence of the inclemency of the weather they decided to have them in some public building; and Faneuil Hall was selected as the most appropriate place.

Upon the platform were seated a large number of distinguished officials and others, who were specially invited to be present. Among these were His Excellency Governor Talbot, Hon. A. W. Beard, Collector of the Port, Hon. E. S. Tobey, Postmaster of Boston, Hon. Geo. P. Sanger, U.S. District Attorney, Hon. John P. Healy, City Solicitor, Hon. Josiah Quincy, and other past Mayors of Boston, Hon. Geo. Washington Warren, Hon. D. K. Hitchcock, the members of the City Council, and many representatives of the clergy and the bar.

The Rev. Phillips Brooks offered the following

PRAYER.

O Father of mercies and God of all comfort, we invoke Thy blessing on the celebration which has called us here to-day.

We thank Thee for all that this celebration means: for a race set free, for a country at peace, and for Lincoln at rest from his labors. Among the memories of the past we stand and offer Thee our humble gratitude for all the mercies of prosperity and freedom which Thou hast sent to us; and since, in the mysteriousness of Thy government, these mercies could not come to us except through war and terrible distress, we thank Thee even for the fearful struggle which our hearts remember as if it were a thing of yesterday.

We praise Thee for all the patriotic and heroic dead. Thou didst incorporate the principles for which our land contended in noble men who freely gave their lives for freedom and their country. For all of them we thank Thee, and especially for him who stands preëminent among them, — the man of conscience, and reverence, and trust, of faith and hope and charity, of simplicity and truthfulness in life, of faithfulness to death. We bless Thee that his character stands forever to represent the best character of the country that was saved from ruin and of the men who saved her.

And, now, we thank Thee at last his name and life have found a perpetual memorial in this city. Thou hast put it into the heart of Thy servant to set up this statue for a perpetual token of the nobleness of self-sacrifice, and of the gratitude of a redeemed and liberated people.

We solemnly dedicate the statue which he has built to liberty and patriotism, to the love of man and to the fear of Thee. May the men and women and children who pass under its shadow hear its voice telling them the story of the sad, brave, blessed life of Lincoln, so that his memory may be an everlasting inspiration to us all.

For while we thank Thee for the past we crave Thy blessing for the years to come ; while we honor the dead, the tasks that the living must do are waiting at our hands. Be Thou the Guide and Master of our governors. In this land where all are governors be Thou the Guide and Master of us all. Keep us all true to the duty, little or great, which Thou hast given us, pure from all corruption, strong against all temptation, full of most humble humility before Thee, and of a brave and tender love for fellow-man, such as there was in him whose statue we dedicate and whose memory we revere to-day.

So may peace and happiness, truth and justice, religion and piety, be established among us for all generations.

These things and all else that Thou seest that we need, we ask in all humility in the name of Jesus Christ our Lord. Amen.

POEM.

BY JOHN G. WHITTIER.

Amidst thy sacred effigies
    Of old renown give place,
O city, Freedom-loved! to his
    Whose hand unchained a race.

Take the worn frame, that rested not
    Save in a martyr's grave —
The care-lined face, that none forgot,
    Bent to the kneeling slave.

Let man be free! The mighty word
    He spake was not his own;
An impulse from the Highest stirred
    These chiselled lips of stone.

The cloudy sign, the fiery guide,
    Along his pathway ran,
And Nature, through his voice, denied
    The ownership of man.

We rest in peace where these sad eyes
    Saw peril, strife, and pain:
His was the nation's sacrifice,
    And ours the priceless gain.

O symbol of God's will on earth
    As it is done above!
Bear witness to the cost and worth
    Of justice and of love.

Stand in thy place and testify
    To coming ages long,
That truth is stronger than a lie,
    And righteousness than wrong.

This was written for the occasion by Mr. Whittier, and was read by Master Andrew Chamberlain, a graduate of the Boston Latin School.

Alderman Charles H. B. Breck, chairman of the committee, then presented the completed work to the Mayor.

ALDERMAN BRECK'S ADDRESS.

Mr. Mayor: — We are here to-day to dedicate a group of statuary donated to the City of Boston by our distinguished and esteemed fellow-citizen, the Hon. Moses Kimball, whose liberal generosity is most warmly appreciated, and will be remembered by not only this, but by each succeeding generation of Bostonians.

Much well-deserved credit is due to Mr. Kimball for the nice discriminating taste and excellent judgment that prompted him in the selection of a gift so beautiful, so appropriate, and so suggestive of historical reminiscences, as this group of emblematical figures, representing the most interesting, the most important, and the most sublime event that has ever transpired in the history of the world, resulting in the freedom of more than three millions of the colored race, who had been held in the cruel bondage of slavery since the early settlement of our country.

This group will be a lasting memorial of the issuing of that proclamation by Abraham Lincoln which

finally brought about the entire abolition of slavery,
never again, we trust, to be revived in these United
States. The statue of Mr. Lincoln, so expressive and
life-like, will ever remind us of the amiable disposition and many noble virtues of that eminently good
and great man, and will always be dearly cherished
by a truly grateful people, who for long years had
wept and prayed that the curse of slavery, with all its
attendant cruelties and horrors, might be done away
with. Through many differences of opinions, both
political and social, and the intervention of powerful
family and private interests, this could not be accom-
plished until President Lincoln, when all other measures had failed to bring to an end the most disastrous
and terrible civil war the world had ever known,
on the first of January, 1863, issued his proclamation
of emancipation, which hastened the close of the war
and foreshadowed the coming of liberty to the down-
trodden and oppressed.

But it is not for me, Mr. Mayor, to enlarge on this
subject. That pleasant duty devolves upon you, and
there is no one more capable or more able to do justice to the occasion than yourself.

As chairman of the joint special committee to
whom was assigned this matter, and as the duly authorized representative of the municipal government,
I now have the honor to surrender to you, Mr. Mayor,

for the citizens of Boston, this elegant work of art.
It will be a most valuable addition to the many beautiful statues that already adorn our avenues and public grounds, and an honor to the donor.

The Mayor received the gift in behalf of the city, and
pronounced the following oration.

The exercises were closed with a benediction by Rev.
Phillips Brooks.

ORATION,

FREDERICK O. PRINCE,

MAYOR.

Gentlemen of the City Council: —

FELLOW-CITIZENS, — We place to-day upon its
pedestal this pleasing work of art, presented to the
City of Boston by our fellow-citizen, the Honorable
MOSES KIMBALL. The Municipal Council and the
people are grateful to the munificent donor, and I
have been requested to express their acknowledg-
ments, and make such dedicatory remarks as seem
appropriate to the occasion.

Mr. Kimball has attached a condition to his gift.
He requires the city to make provision for its care
and protection, and place it where the people "most
do congregate," that they may be constantly re-
minded of the great event it commemorates; for it
is his desire, by this memorial bronze, not only to
adorn the city and gratify our sense of the beautiful,
but to elevate and instruct the popular mind by its

solemn lessons of justice, philanthropy, and patriotism. Thus, in making the gift and directing its location, his liberality and wisdom are equally conspicuous.

The city has agreed to comply with this condition. The site selected is a thoroughfare, and meets the approbation of the considerate donor. May this eloquent memorial endure as long as things made by human hands are permitted to endure; as long as the human mind retains its capacity to know that liberty is the gift of Heaven to man, and that resistance to tyranny is obedience to God.

The desire to record important events, and the great actors therein, by some artistic expression, is such a natural disposition, that all nations, civilized and barbaric, have invoked architecture, sculpture, painting, and poetry, to commemorate their eminent sovereigns, soldiers, statesmen, philosophers, orators, poets, and those who have rendered beneficial service to the State and to humanity. Gratitude, pride, and affection, are not satisfied to trust such commemoration to a vehicle so uncertain as tradition. The historic page informs only the student and the lettered; but all can read and understand, with more or less appreciation, the language of art. The popular mind comprehends more readily an idea in the concrete than the abstract,—an idea expressed

by sensuous forms than by words, however eloquent.
Art performs its highest office when it perpetuates
heroic action. National monuments are epic lessons
to future generations. They instruct, admonish, de-
light, and inspire. That which we dedicate to-day
speaks of the most important act in our annals, and
commemorates one of the great eras of the Republic,
— the *emancipation of four millions of slaves!*

It is fitting and appropriate that we should come
here to Faneuil Hall and have our dedicatory exercises. The associations of this venerable and historic place accord with the solemn character of the
occasion. The walls which heard those denuncia-
tions of tyranny that led to the immortal declaration
— "All men are created free," — should echo our
thanksgiving that all men throughout our broad domain — of every race and color — are at last free,
and witness the consecration of the sculpture which
commemorates the event.

SLAVERY NOW INDEFENSIBLE.

The occasion does not require me to enter at
length into the causes which led to the great civil
war. I do not propose to discuss the right, moral or
legal, of one man to have property in another; nor
shall I have much to say upon the nature and influence of slavery, or the political or economic conse-

quences which have come from it. The opinions of
mankind upon the whole matter have been made up,
and are not to be changed. However much men
may differ as to forms of government, and the
administration of government, whatever divergence
of opinion may exist touching political measures and
political instrumentalities, no one in any part of the
world enlightened by Christian civilization will now
dare to defend slavery as a system of labor. It has
ceased to be ; but its death-struggles convulsed the
country as nothing else could, and provoked the
most dreadful of all wars, — civil war. Let it be
forgotten and buried with the dead past; and in its
grave let us put all the wild passions and bitter animosities it evoked. It was hostile to national union
and domestic peace ; but, now that its baleful influence is over, let us hope that we may be again one
people, politically and socially, so that we may be
the better able to work out our destiny and mission
among the nations of the earth. I propose to recall
to your attention at this time some of the causes
which led to emancipation.

When the Declaration of American Independence
was promulgated all the thirteen colonies were slave-
holding States. At the North it was generally believed that the proposition therein set forth, that all
men were born free, applied alike to the negro as

well as to the white man. In Massachusetts the
Supreme Court, reflecting the sentiments of the
Puritans and their steady devotion to the right of
personal liberty in all men, declared that not only the
slaves here were emancipated by that instrument,
but that they had been already made free, by the
adoption of the State Constitution and Bill of
Rights, previous to the formation of the Federal
Constitution.

In other Northern States similar judicial decisions
were made, and slavery soon ceased to exist therein.
It was otherwise at the South. The material prosperity of that portion of the country was thought to
depend upon the maintenance of slavery, for the time
at least; and, influenced by their supposed interests,
our southern brethren did not consider the declaration as universal in its operation, and therefore re-
stricted its application to white citizens alone.

Whoever inquires into the opinions and sentiments
of the leading minds of the country when the Federal Constitution was formed will find that slavery
was regarded everywhere as a political, if the enlightened sense of the people had not then begun to
consider it as a moral, evil. Thinking men, North
and South, believed its existence was a source of
national weakness, and that its influence on free
labor was unwholesome and depressing. Its ultimate

extinction was therefore desired and expected. Both sections of the country deprecated the continuance of the African slave-trade, from fear that the institution would be perpetuated to an indefinite period; for the belief obtained that slavery would die out if the slave-trade were abandoned.

OPINIONS OF THE EARLY SOUTHERN STATESMEN.

As early as 1772 the Legislature of Virginia had memorialized the King of Great Britain upon the dangers of slavery, and expressed the desire that the slave-trade might be abolished; but the king replied, " that, upon pain of his highest displeasure, the importation of slaves should not be in any respect obstructed." How are we to reconcile this declaration from the crown with the decision of the English court in 1772, in the celebrated Sommersett case, that no man could make a slave of another? Well may honest Ben Franklin indignantly say, " Pharisaical Britain! to pride thyself in setting free a single slave that happened to land on thy coast, while thy laws continue a traffic whereby so many thousands are dragged into a slavery that is entailed upon their posterity."

As I have said, it was thought that slavery would soon die out if the importation of slaves should cease. When it was proposed in the Federal Con-

vention by some northern delegates that the slave-
trade should continue beyond the term of twenty
years, the southern members objected that the period
was too long. Mr. Madison was strongly of this
opinion, and so expressed himself. Jefferson said
during the war of the Revolution, "The way, I
hope, is preparing, under the auspices of Heaven, for
a total emancipation." At another time he confessed
that "he trembled for his country when he remembered
that God was just." Washington declared, "there
was not a man living who wished more sincerely than
he to see a plan adopted for the abolition of slavery."
Luther Martin and William Pinckney, the great law-
yers of Maryland, both advocated emancipation, —
the former in the Federal Convention of 1787, and
the latter in the Maryland House of Delegates in
1789. Mr. Iredell, of North Carolina, said in the
Constitutional Convention, "When the entire abolition of slavery takes place, it will be an event which
must be pleasing to every generous mind, and to
every friend of human nature." I might quote the
opinions of many other southern statesmen of that
day to the same effect. Mr. Webster observes in his
great speech on the Constitution and the Union,
"that the eminent men, the most eminent men, and
nearly all the conspicuous politicians of the South,
then held the same sentiments, — that slavery was an

evil, a blight, a scourge, and a curse. There are no
terms of reprobation of slavery so vehement in the
North at that day as in the South. The North was
not so excited against it as the South; and the reason is, I suppose, that there was much less of it at
the North, and the people did not see, or think they
saw, the evils so prominently as they were seen, or
thought to be seen, at the South."

Reverdy Johnson, Senator from Maryland, in his
memorable speech made on the 5th April, 1864, in the
Senate of the United States, on the constitutional
amendment abolishing slavery, said, "The men
who fought through the Revolution, those who
survived its perils and shared its glory, and who
were called to the convention by which the Constitution of the United States was drafted and rec-
ommended to the adoption of the American people,
almost without exception thought that slavery was
not only an evil to any people among whom it might
exist, but that it was an evil of the highest character,
which it was the duty of all Christian people, if possible, to remove, because it was a sin as well as an
evil. I think the history of those times will bear me
out in the statement, that if the men by whom the
Constitution was framed, and the people by whom it
was adopted, had anticipated the time in which we
live, they would have provided by constitutional enact-

ment that that evil and that sin should at some comparatively unremote day be removed; . . . they earnestly desired, not only upon grounds of political economy, not only upon reasons material in their character, but upon grounds of morality and religion, that sooner or later the institution should terminate." As further evidence of the state of public opinion contemporaneous with the formation of the Constitution, I will add, that abolition societies were then formed in most of the original thirteen States; in Rhode Island, Connecticut, Maryland, Virginia, Delaware, New York, and Pennsylvania. That of the latter was formed as early as 1774, and Dr. Franklin was its president. John Jay, Chief Justice of the Supreme Court of the United States, was the first, and Hamilton was the second, president of the New York society.

But the most striking proof of the unanimity of public sentiment throughout the country, South as well as North, in regard to the ultimate extinction of slavery, is to be found in the passage of the celebrated ordinance of 1787, by which slavery was forever excluded "from the whole territory over which the Congress of the United States had jurisdiction." And that was all the territory north-west of the Ohio. *This ordinance was passed by the unanimous concurrence of the whole South.* The vote of every

State in the Union was given in its favor, with the exception of a single individual vote, which was given by a *northern* man. "The ordinance," says Mr. Webster, "prohibiting slavery forever northwest of the Ohio has the hand and seal of every southern member of Congress."

PROVISIONS OF THE CONSTITUTION.

Notwithstanding these views of the southern people touching slavery as an institution, at the time the fathers were engaged in framing the Federal Constitution, they were not prepared for immediate emancipation. Objections were urged against it. It was thought that the economic interests of the South would suffer, for a time at least, by any such sweeping and radical change in their system of labor, and they were unwilling to risk the experiment. Guarantees for the protection of slavery were therefore demanded as the condition upon which they would adopt the political compact which was to "form a more perfect union," and make us one people.

There was much embarrassment in adjusting the matter so as to satisfy all parties. An agreement, however, was finally reached through mutual compromises, and the Constitution was ratified and adopted by all the States.

Three important propositions were thus established: —

First. — The recognition of slavery as it then existed in the States, with full power in the States over slavery within their respective limits.

Second. — The prohibition of slavery in all the territory then owned by the United States, through the adoption of the ordinance of 1787.

Third. — The grant to the new government of the power to abolish the slave-trade after a limited period.

The ratification of the Constitution was concurrence on the part of both North and South in these different propositions.

The new government being thus established, the United States of America took a new departure, and entered the family of nations as one sovereign power, formed from many parts, and commenced a new career of national life.

It had the blessings and prayers of all those in every quarter of the globe who love liberty, and who feel that civilization can only develop and advance under its benign influence. The future seemed surely " full of joy and promise and sunshine." The genius of the people, their ardent love of liberty, their hardy virtues, their indomitable courage, ever reliable for the defence of their political rights, their

form of government so admirably adapted for the
development of all that makes a nation powerful and
prosperous, their varied climate, their vast resources,
their fortunate geographical position, with the wide
Atlantic between them and the old feudal world, and
the national polity inspired by the genius of Washington, which avoided all entangling alliances, — all
promised centuries of happy, prosperous, and glorious
national life.   The Saturnian age was to return
again.

But there were those whose judgments were not
wholly controlled by these high hopes and pleasing
anticipations.   They saw, from the beginning, beneath
the surface of this halcyon sea, and not far below it,
hidden and dangerous rocks that lay in the path of
the ship of state.   They felt that the government,
with all its apparent exemption from the causes of
national decline and decay, with all its seeming pos-
session of assured and immortal life, was, like the
divinely born Grecian hero, vulnerable in one place
at least, — in that feature of its organization which
compelled the recognition and protection of slavery.
They could not see how such potent antagonisms as
Slavery and Freedom could long continue to exist side
by side; and they felt that, sooner or later, either the
encroaching freedom of the North must dominate
the South, or the encroaching slavery of the South

must dominate the North, despite of covenants, compromises, compacts, and constitutions.

THE IRREPRESSIBLE CONFLICT.

The event corresponded with their predictions. " No great political or moral revolution," says a distinguished essayist, "has ever occurred, which has not been accompanied by its prognostic." Such soon appeared, foreshowing the great change which was to come over the southern mind with respect, not only to the policy of maintaining slavery as a system of labor, but to the moral right to do so. Cotton, which was not considered a commercial product of the South at the adoption of the Constitution, was found, after the invention of the cotton gin, so adapted to the climate of the slave States as practically to give them a monopoly of its cultivation. It was soon discovered that here was an inexhaustible mine of wealth. All that was needed for its development was cheap labor, and it was believed that such could be only found in slave labor. The entire policy of the South in respect to the institution immediately changed, and all their thoughts and efforts were directed to its protection and extension. For this purpose new territories were acquired and new States admitted into the Union. The political power of the South was thus greatly augmented, and the North, alarmed lest slavery should be nationalized, organized to prevent its further extension.

These two opposing forces soon generated an
" irrepressible conflict."

Both sides complained of each other.   Each
charged broken faith and violations of the constitutional compact.   When time shall soften the prejudices and calm the passions engendered in the
unnatural strife, so that the conduct of both parties
can be examined with judicial impartiality, the historian will be able to set forth all the facts and make
up the record.   We are too near the events; we
share too largely, both at the North and the South,
the feelings and opinions which inaugurated the
strife, to enable us to make proper discrimination.
The verdict must be rendered by another generation;
but there is one fact about which there can be no
dispute.   The South, alleging that slavery and their
interests were endangered by the election of Mr.
Lincoln to the Presidency, and the access to power
of the Republican party, and claiming the right of
secession, made war upon the flag.   Thereupon, the
administration, in obedience to the mandates of the
Constitution, marshalled its forces for the maintenance of the Federal authority and the preservation
of the Union.   Civil war was thus inaugurated.

Among the questions involved in this terrible controversy, which the student of history may perhaps raise, will be, whether this conflict could have been avoided by any different statesmanship, notwithstanding the intense feeling respecting slavery which divided the people of the two sections, and the hostile spirit which animated them.

It may be asked, if slavery be regarded as the predisponent, as well as the immediate cause of the war, whether it would not ere long have died out under the advancing civilization of the age, which was fast destroying the conditions under which it could alone exist? Would not the progress of moral ideas, and the enlightened opinions of mankind, have made it impossible for any nation, especially the English-speaking race, to uphold forever the hideous institution?

Data might perhaps be found for such speculation in the changed sentiments of the northern tier of slave States during the decade preceding the war, touching the right to hold property in man, and the policy of maintaining this system of labor, and in the significant fact that the slaves were fast disappearing from this section of the country. The recent action of Russia, Spain, Brazil, and other nations, might be cited to show the great changes in public opinion in respect to the institution. In Cuba all slaves over sixty years of age have been manu-

mitted; and within a few days the Spanish Minister
of Colonies presented to the Senate at Madrid the
government bill, touching the abolition of slavery in
Cuba, remarking that "it was contrary to the laws
of nature, and could no longer be maintained in the
civilized world." Surely, the world moves! Perhaps
it will be found, upon careful examination of all the
facts, that slavery was rather the exciting than the
actual cause of the strife between the North and the
South, and that deeper down there were the same
forces at work for the accomplishment of this result,
which threatened nullification and secession in 1830,
and which would have then led to civil war but
for the eloquence of Webster, and the firmness of
Jackson.

LINCOLN NOT AN EXTREMIST.

Mr. Lincoln, when elected President of the United
States, was not an abolitionist in the extreme sense
of the term. He was not of the *higher-law* party.
He was opposed to slavery — morally and politically.
He believed the Declaration of Independence oper-
ated equally upon all men, without regard to color;
and while he was opposed to the extension of slavery
into new States and territories, he recognized fully
the binding force of the compromises under which
the Constitution was adopted, and the protection

which that compact gave slavery in the States where
it existed. He had no disposition or intention to
molest or interfere in any way with the institution
there. He repeatedly defined his position on this
question in his speeches in the political campaigns
previous to his election, and so clearly and unam-
biguously that he could not be misunderstood.

In the celebrated debate with Mr. Douglas, when
they were both candidates for the United States
Senate, Judge Douglas asked him whether he then
stood, as he stood in 1854, in favor of the unconditional repeal of the fugitive slave law; and he replied, "I do not now nor ever did stand in favor of
the unconditional repeal of the fugitive slave law."
Judge Douglas then asked him if he stood pledged,
as in 1854, against the admission of any more slave
States into the Union; and he answered, "I do not
now nor ever did stand pledged against the admission of any more slave States." He further said that
he was not pledged to the abolition of slavery in the
District of Columbia, nor to the prohibition of the
slave-trade between the States.

These declarations were not satisfactory to the
radical anti-slavery men; for they showed most con-
clusively that he did not belong to that political
church.

In his address at Cincinnati, in 1859, he said, "I

am not what they call, as I understand it, a black
Republican, but I think slavery wrong, morally and
politically;" and, referring to some Kentuckians present, observed, "We Republicans mean to treat you,
as near as we possibly can, as Washington, Jefferson,
and Madison, treated you. We mean to leave you
alone, and in no way interfere with your institution;
to abide by all and every compromise of the Constitution."

In his remarks to the Mayor and Common Council
of Washington, just after his election as President,
he assured them that the people should have all
their rights; "not grudgingly, but fully and fairly."

In his first inaugural, and in his proclamation, he
says, "Apprehension seems to exist among the
people of the Southern States, that by the accession
of a Republican administration their property and
their peace and personal security are to be endangered. There never has been any reasonable
cause for such apprehension. Indeed, the most
ample evidence to the contrary has all the while
existed, and been open to their inspection. It is
found in nearly all the published speeches of him
who now addresses you. I do but quote from one
of those speeches when I declare, that 'I have no
purpose, directly or indirectly, to interfere with the
institution of slavery in the States where it now

exists.' I believe I have no lawful right to do so, and I have no inclination to do so. Those who nominated and elected me did so with the full knowledge that I had made this and similar declarations, and had never recanted them; and, more than this, they placed in the platform for my acceptance, and as a law to themselves and to me, the clear and emphatic resolution which I now read: —

"'*Resolved,* That the maintenance inviolate of the rights of the States, and especially of the rights of each State, to order and control its own domestic institutions according to its own judgment exclusively, is essential to that balance of power on which the perfection and endurance of our political fabric depends; and we denounce the lawless invasion by armed force of the soil of any State or territory, no matter under what pretext, as among the gravest crimes.'

"I now reiterate these sentiments, and in doing so I only press upon the public attention the most conclusive evidence of which the case is susceptible, that the property, peace, and security, of no section are to be in anywise endangered by the now incoming administration."

THE POSITION OF THE REPUBLICAN PARTY.

Whatever the South may have feared from the

extreme men around Mr. Lincoln, they had, or could
have had, no apprehension that he would not stand
squarely and firmly by his opinions and promises on
this great question; for if there was .any trait of
character, any one virtue, for which he was especially noted, it was his honesty and fidelity to truth.
These qualities were conspicuous through all his
checkered and unblemished life, from the time when,
poor and struggling for existence, he followed the
hard fortunes of the flat-boatman on the Mississippi;
through all his honorable career as a lawyer and a
legislator, until elected to the highest office in the
gift of the people.   When he took the oath upon his
inauguration to "preserve, protect, and defend, the
Constitution of the United States," he took it, as he
says, "with no mental reservations, and with no
purpose to construe the Constitution or laws by any
hypercritical rules." Can any one doubt that he
intended from the beginning to keep this solemn
oath, and to administer the government honestly,
fairly, and according to the requirements of the
Constitution?

It is thus evident that there was no design on the
part of the Republican party to interfere, upon their
accession to power, with slavery in the States where
it then existed. Furthermore, if they had such design they could not have executed it. Gov. Perry,

of South Carolina, well said, "The rights of the South were in no possible danger, even had Mr. Lincoln been disposed to interfere with them. There was at that time a majority of twenty-seven in the House of Representatives politically opposed to him. There was a majority in the Senate of six opposed to him. A majority of the Supreme Court were opposed to the principles of the Republican party. A large majority of the people had supported others for the Presidency. He was powerless to injure the slave States." Some of the more radical members of the party might have proposed, in their hostility to the institution, violent and unconstitutional measures; but they were inconsiderable in numbers and without controlling influence.

It was the duty of the government to defend itself against all assaults of its enemies, foreign and domestic,—to maintain the Union of the States,—and it was bound to use all powers and means within its control necessary for the purpose. When, therefore, the war came, the executive summoned the military force of the country for its protection; but it was not until the contest had continued for nearly two years; until a vast amount of treasure and blood had been expended, and it had been proved that the armies of the republic were inadequate for the suppression of this gigantic revolt, that the President, as a last resource, adopted the expedient of emancipation.

All his conduct shows that, in taking this important step, Mr. Lincoln did not move hastily, like a partisan, who was impatiently seeking for the opportunity to abolish slavery; but slowly, cautiously, and reluctantly, as a statesman should, who appreciated the solemn magnitude of the measure, and saw the momentous consequences which would follow it. He reflected long and seriously before acting. He conscientiously considered the obligations of his official oath and the demands of duty.

THE POSTPONEMENT OF EMANCIPATION.

No political, party, or other improper considerations were permitted to influence his judgment or control his action. So careful was he not to err in the matter, it was thought by many, not extreme in their views, that the cause of the Union suffered by his delay. But in so grave an exigency he preferred to err on what he deemed the safest side. When therefore General Fremont issued his order, in August, 1861, declaring the slaves of the Missouri insurgents to be thereafter free, Lincoln, regarding the measure premature and impolitic, although he believed it was competent to adopt it under the war powers of the Constitution, did not then think it an "indispensable necessity," and directed its modification.

When, a little later, General Cameron, the Secretary of War, suggested the arming of the negroes, he did not think this an "indispensable necessity," and objected to the proposal.

When, still later, General Hunter made his proclamation and order declaring all the slaves in South Carolina, Georgia, and Florida free forever, he annulled it, "not thinking the indispensable necessity had come." On the question of emancipating and arming negroes, he said, "The Union must be preserved, and all indispensable means must be used; but I deprecate haste in the use of extreme measures, which might reach the loyal as well as the disloyal."

It will be remembered that the public sentiment was becoming daily more and more intense in the demand for immediate and unconditional emancipation as the shortest and surest way of bringing the war to an end. It was urged that the crushing of slavery would be the crushing of the rebellion. It was claimed that emancipation would bring into the Union ranks hundreds of thousands of colored men. The more violent of the Republican newspapers denounced Mr. Lincoln for remissness and inaction. He replied in his defence, "My paramount object is to save the Union, and not either to save or destroy

slavery.   If I could save the Union, without freeing
any slave, I would do it; if I could save it by freeing
all the slaves I would do it; and if I could save it by
freeing some, and leaving others alone, I would do
it."

Notwithstanding all the pressure upon him for the
issue of the Proclamation of Emancipation, he still
hastens slowly. He waits until he could put the
slave party clearly in the wrong; until the South
had passed the Rubicon; until it was evident that
the insurgents would never abandon the contest; until the war had been so waged as to leave no alterna-
tive but to yield the cause, and allow the Union to
be broken up and destroyed.

I recall all this to your attention to show how
carefully and cautiously he reached his determination to adopt the measure of emancipation. When
he finally resolved upon it he gave ample notice of
his intention, that those who would be affected by its
operation might save themselves, if they wished to
do so. After months went by, with no signs of surrender, and no indication that the enemies of the
Union and the republic would return to their alle-
giance, declaring that "he sincerely believed it to be
an act of justice, warranted by the Constitution upon
military necessity, upon which he invoked the considerate judgment of mankind and the gracious favor

of Almighty God," he issued the Proclamation of Emancipation.

The bolt was launched which was certain to end the war, destroy secession, vindicate the national authority, and save the Union.

EMANCIPATION A WAR MEASURE.

It is not necessary to consider the right of government to resort to emancipation as a war measure. I will only briefly say, that it is not to be denied that, under the circumstances, it was fitting and proper; that it was, as Mr. Lincoln said, justified as a military necessity. It was approved by Congress by a resolution passed by a large majority, and the country has endorsed it.

War existed between the United States and the seceding States; and the Supreme Court of the United States held, in 1863, in the case of the Hiawatha, "that where the course of justice is interrupted by revolt, rebellion, or insurrection, so that the courts of justice cannot be kept open, civil war exists, and hostilities may be prosecuted on the same footing as if those opposing the government were foreign enemies. All persons residing in the insurgent States are liable to be treated as enemies. . . . They are none the less enemies because they are traitors."

By the laws of war, the property of both enemies

and friends may be taken when needed. If slaves
were property, then the government could by these
laws take them to help subdue the enemy; their lib-
eration would obviously weaken the latter and
strengthen the former. The Constitution gives the
Executive belligerent powers *flagrante bello*, and he
is the sole judge whether the exigency exists for the
exercise of these powers. The only limit to the war
powers is to be found in the law of nations; and by
the law of nations, and the practice of belligerents
in modern times, the slaves of an enemy may be liberated in time of war by military power. This
power was exercised by England in the revolution-
ary war, and in the State of Virginia alone more
than thirty thousand slaves were thus liberated.
Jefferson himself conceded that England had this
right. England again exercised this right in the
war of 1812. France did the same in her wars with
England, and some of the South American republics
have also exercised this right, and it has been recognized and admitted by all publicists. I do not understand that it is denied at the South.

It may be asked, whether it was *expedient* and
politic to issue the proclamation. If we recur to
the condition of things at the time, the question will
be readily answered. The government had been
trying for nearly two years to subdue the rebellion.

Immense sums of money had been expended. Many hundred thousand soldiers had been called out. Many fierce and sanguinary battles had been fought. The war had assumed gigantic proportions, and extended over a vast area of territory. Eleven States were in revolt. All their resources of men and money were levied. The "cradle and the grave" had been robbed for recruits. The most inflexible determination had been everywhere shown to surrender only when conquered. Foreign intervention was threatened. It may be doubted whether the Union could be saved by the means within the control of the government unless the enemy were deprived of the aid of the slaves, — for the latter were a great source of power; they raised the supplies for carrying on hostilities; they constructed military works, and served in the armies. Emancipation would transfer these allies to the national flag, and strengthen the national ranks by vast numbers of willing recruits. There can be no doubt, then, that it was our *policy*, as it was our right, to proclaim freedom to the negroes.

EFFECT OF THE PROCLAMATION.

Once free they could not be again enslaved, for the right of the slave to his freedom after being liberated is not to be disputed; and, furthermore, it would

be most atrocious as well as unjust, that he who had
once worn the uniform of a United States soldier,
and carried the flag through the carnage of battle,
should be again enslaved upon the recurrence of the
peace which he had helped to conquer. It may be
here observed that the Confederate Congress, in the
last hours of the war, passed a bill authorizing the
employment of slaves as soldiers, although the measure was adopted too late to help their cause. But in
the debate upon the bill it was conceded that " to
arm the negroes is to give them freedom. When
they come out scarred from the conflict they must be
free."

Furthermore, it is not to be denied that the government is at all times entitled to the aid of all those
it protects in its hour of danger. The black man is
as much bound as the white man to perform military
duty. There is no discrimination. When the common safety is imperilled, all alike must respond to
the call of patriotism.

The sequel demonstrated the wisdom of emancipation. As soon as the proclamation was issued, the
power of the rebellion was broken. The capacity
of the insurgents to continue the contest weakened,
and was soon destroyed. Both parties soon saw that
further resistance to the national arms could not
long be maintained. Emancipation, by thus short-

ening the war, saved thousands of lives, and a vast increase of national debt.

RIGHT OF SECESSION.

It should be remembered that the Southerners always denied that they were revolutionists. They justified, or attempted to justify, their action in taking arms against the government, by the right of secession, which, through their interpretation of the Federal Constitution, belonged to all the States.

It was claimed that, after the passage of the secession ordinances by the slave States, the latter resumed all the sovereignty which they possessed before the adoption of the Constitution, and that when they united and established the Southern Confederacy, it became *de jure* — as it was during the years of the war *de facto* — an independent autonomy; that upon this theory the contest was not a rebellion, but a war between two nationalities. Beyond question a large part of the southern people honestly believed in this alleged right of secession. Their political leaders, of the school of Haynes and Calhoun, had long maintained the construction of the Constitution which gave this right, and the public mind in that section of the country had become so thoroughly imbued and saturated with this heresy

that the people were united and fixed in their determination to maintain this right.

We of the North, under the teachings of our
statesmen, denied that a State, for any cause, could
secede. We are especially indebted to Daniel Webster for our political instruction and guidance here.
Previous to his masterly exposition of the nature
and genius of the Federal Constitution, the character
of that instrument, and its effects upon the States,
and the relation of the States to each other and to
the central government, and the respective rights and
obligations of each, were imperfectly understood.
He demonstrated that this political compact established something more than a confederation. He
proved, to the people of the North at least, that it
created a national unity, and established a national
government, notwithstanding it reserved to the States
certain powers and remains of sovereignty for the
control of their local and domestic affairs; and that
the union thus created could not be dissolved except
by the consent of all the States or by revolution.

This exposition was generally accepted by the
country north of the slave line, and fostered, if it did
not create, that patriotic and national sentiment to
which appeal was so successfully made when the flag
was assailed and the war inaugurated. The whole
North being a unit against secession, all its patri-

otism was aroused, and all its vast resources of men, money, and military material contributed to the cause without stint. Every draft upon its loyalty for the defence of the government and the maintenance of the Union was recognized.

It may be doubted whether there would have been this unanimity of sentiment in respect to the rights of the general government, or the same inflexible determination to maintain them, if the war of secession had come upon our country at an earlier period of our history, and before the theory of *nationality* had fully formed and crystallized.

When we consider how fixed the two sections were in their convictions touching their constitutional rights, and remember the intensity of the popular feeling therein; the fierce invective of the press; the acrimony of Congressional debate, and all the circumstances which surrounded and controlled the question, — it is evident that its peaceful solution could hardly be expected; that compromise was almost impossible; that the Gordian knot could not be untied, and was to be cut by the sword.

THE DECISION OF THE WAR.

The war has decided that there shall be no question or differences of opinion as to the loyalty due from the States and from the people to the national

government. It has decided that there is no right
of secession. It has decided that slavery, which
prompted the assertion of this right, shall cease to
exist.

These decisions will never be disturbed. They are
final and irreversible. The dogma of secession was
the logical sequence of the doctrine of strict construction. The advocates of the latter maintained
the absurd proposition, that the framers of a constitution for the formation " of a more perfect union "
contrived such a monstrosity as a government without the powers necessary for its existence; that they
called into being an entity incapable of maintaining
itself against the revolt of its own parts, — a creation
which might be destroyed, like the children of Sat-
urn, as soon as born; a something that might at once
become a nothing.

If this be so, then all the time and labor of the
constitutional convention were expended in vain, for
its boasted work is of little value. What folly to
adopt a national flag, and demand for the United
States a place among the sovereignties of the world,
if any State, or any number of States, could at
pleasure break up the government and destroy its
unity and individuality!

But the framers of the Constitution were wise men,
and understood government as a science. By this

instrument they gave the federation all powers of a national character for the enforcement of national authority, and thus provided for the preservation of the Union. "Perpetuity," says Mr. Lincoln, "is implied, if not expressed, in the fundamental law of all national governments."

But while the rights of the national government have been adjusted, and the powers which properly belong to it recognized, through the arbitrament of war, a grave question looms in the distance, whether, in the flush of victory, it is not disposed to claim more than belongs to it; whether it may not encroach upon those rights which under the Constitution are reserved to the States. The preponderance of the centripetal may work as much of mischief in our political system as that of the centrifugal forces.

Soon after the adoption of the Constitution it was provided by amendment, "that the powers not delegated to the United States by the Constitution, nor prohibited by it to the States, are reserved to the States respectively or to the people." Our political system, as the Supreme Court of the United States has well said, "is an indestructible union composed of indestructible States." In the distribution of national and State powers we should watch with equal vigilance, that the rights and powers of the federal government are not disturbed by the States,

and that the rights and powers of the States are not
disturbed by the government. A just equilibrium
between both is essential for the protection of both.
Power ever seeks to augment itself. The path of
history is strewn with the wreck of governments
once free, which have been destroyed by executive
usurpation. To establish the just authority of the
national government we have expended thousands of
millions of treasure and fought hundreds of battles.
Let us take care that in avoiding one extreme we
do not drift into another, which may require like
sacrifices to correct. Our national safety lies in the
middle path. If the general government is permitted to usurp the reserved rights of the States
in matters of local and domestic concern, where the
latter have exclusive cognizance, each act of usurpation will become the precedent for another. Encroachment will follow encroachment, until the
harmony of the system is destroyed, and the government perverted from a union of coördinate and
coequal parts, each recognizing its loyal obligations
to the Union, and the Union in turn protecting the
rights of each, into a centralized and consolidated
authority, which will ultimately assert imperial sway,
to the destruction of constitutional government, and
the overthrow of free institutions. An "indestructible union of indestructible States" will give peace,

prosperity, and glory. The States, free and independent in their own spheres, and in the enjoyment of their just rights, will revolve in their appropriate orbits around the common centre of the national government, whose attracting and repelling forces, so adjusted as to maintain their proper influences over each portion of the system, will keep the whole in subordinate and harmonious relations.

EMANCIPATION MARKS A NATIONAL ERA.

The abolition of slavery may be said to make one of our national eras. The establishment of American Independence relieved us from the dwarfing influence of colonial dependence and the oppressions of imperial power. The emancipation of four millions of slaves delivered us from a dangerous disease, which threatened the national life. None will deny the baleful influence of slavery. It was an incubus upon the prosperity of the country. It retarded the development of its resources. It depressed values. It degraded labor, and affected injuriously every economic interest. There can be no doubt that the industries of the South were largely stimulated by this system of labor; but I think it can be shown that such prosperity as the slave States enjoyed was not attained by, but in spite of, slavery.

RESULT OF EMANCIPATION.

Now that this cause of evil has been removed we may hope that no great impediment to our advance in all the things which make a nation great and prosperous will be found. There may be sectional rivalries and differences of opinion touching many matters of national concern. The people of different States may not agree as to the policy which should govern in respect to fiscal measures, tariffs, the disposition of public lands, the construction of public works, the acquisition of new territory, the maintenance of armies and navies, and other questions of national polity; but these will be powerless to endanger the national existence; they will not be rocks and shoals to endanger the course of the ship of state, but merely storms through which statesmanship will safely guide and carry it. We may now hope, if we act wisely, for the perpetuity of the Union for as many centuries as the institutions of human contrivance can be expected to endure. The territory we occupy has been so shaped by Providence, its configuration is so peculiar, its mountain ranges and river valleys so formed, as to afford no national boundaries, and compel the Union as a necessity. We cannot divide into separate sovereignties. This natural adhesion is strengthened by the bond to be found in the influence of the Puritan spirit which pervades the country. Two-thirds of our people trace their lineage to the race which landed from the Mayflower. From the lakes to the gulf, and between the two oceans, the public mind and heart are imbued with the great qualities of these heroic men, — their love of liberty, their respect for law, their capacity for labor, their dauntless courage, their self-reliance, and their individuality.

Puritanism absorbs and proselytes. Its characteristics have been forced upon the fifty millions who now occupy our continental domain. We may therefore anticipate a brilliant future. The recuperative powers of the country are everywhere active. The wounds of war are healing. Our vast resources are developing. A million of soldiers have returned to the ranks of civil life, and become producers. The manufacturer, the farmer, the mechanic, all the workers in the various fields of labor, are promoting the national industries. The vast debt incurred in defence of the Union has been largely lessened. Our enormous exports are bringing daily and hourly to our shores the wealth of transatlantic countries. We have only to be true to ourselves, act justly, and cultivate peace, to become the leading nation of the world in all that makes a nation great and prosperous.

But, while we indulge these pleasing anticipations and picture to ourselves the brilliant promises of the political future, let us not forget the claims of the four millions of slaves liberated by the emancipation, symbolized by the bronze we dedicate to-day. Let us not forget that they are now endowed with the same "inalienable rights of life, liberty, and the pursuit of happiness," the same right to enjoy in "safety and tranquillity the blessings of life," which the white man enjoys. Under the amendments of the Constitution they are American citizens, subject to the obligations of citizenship and entitled to its privileges.

Since their manumission they have shown themselves generally disposed to be orderly and well behaved. Their peculiar physical organization requires them to live in the southern climate. They must be, for the most part, agriculturists. Their labor is necessary for the prosperity of the South. Without it the rich lands of that section will depreciate in value, for the white laborers cannot well fill their places. That they are industrious is proved by the fact that the largest crop of southern staples ever raised was gathered the present year. Policy, then, as well as justice, demands the good treatment of the freedmen, the recognition of their rights, and the protection of their interests.

But it is not merely their material welfare which should concern the people of this country. In order to make them good citizens and fit them for the discharge of the duties of citizenship, and especially to fit them for the judicious exercise of the right of suffrage, which has been recently extended to them through the amendments of the Constitution, they should be educated. Not only their own interests demand this, but the national safety calls for it as a necessity.

It is universally admitted that the moral and intellectual education of the people can alone uphold republican institutions. Whatever, then, is done for the elevation of the white should also be done for that of the colored men. They have been called the " wards of the nation." Let the nation treat them with a guardian's care, and see to it that they are trained and educated like other human beings, and taught to be honest, truthful, virtuous, and God-fearing.

The South, because of the poverty resulting from war, cannot, at this time, do all that is necessary in this direction; but the reports of the trustees of the Peabody Education Fund show that it realizes its obligations in the premises, and has made commendable progress in the work.

It is to be hoped that the general government will

soon see that it is its duty, as well as its interest, to aid our southern brethren in their efforts to discharge the solemn responsibilities imposed upon them by emancipation.

PERSONAL CHARACTER OF LINCOLN.

Allow me a few words touching the personal character of Mr. Lincoln. Those who have acted important parts in the drama of public affairs can rarely be justly understood or appreciated by their contemporaries. The latter are too near the scene of events to see them in their just proportions and relations; too greatly affected by the passions engendered in the conflict of opinions to perceive the facts as they exist; too often misled by the prejudices of party spirit to judge motives and measures with the candor which truth demands, and too strongly wedded to favorite theories and preconceived judgments to feel the full force of reason. Great statesmen especially, who have been in advance of their times, and devised governmental polities and systems whose fruition is in the future, have been compelled to look to posterity for appreciation, and, like Bacon, to leave "their names and memories to men's charitable speeches, and to foreign nations and the next age." Hence we find that the opinions touching the public men of preceding generations are often greatly modified when history has gathered all the facts and data — winnowed the true from the false, and made up its record.

There have been, however, exceptional cases where great qualities and splendid achievements have been so conspicuous as to receive at once full popular recognition. Our earlier annals are distinguished by a few of them. Washington and Franklin and Hamilton were all appreciated in their day and generation. We of to-day can add to the illustrious constellation the revered name of Lincoln. His individuality was so marked, his moral and intellectual character so fully recognized, and his motives and conduct so well understood, that all knew and saw him as he was, — a man of strong natural powers of mind, of fixed principles, of great purity of character, and of dauntless moral courage, who hated every species of injustice and wrong. No time is wanted to understand him. No time is required to obliterate blots which impair his fame. There is little in his public conduct to be excused or forgotten. His place in the Pantheon of illustrious benefactors is by general consent assured.

Such is the judgment of to-day, and such will be the judgment of posterity and future ages. Those of the North who were politically opposed to him, and who, under the prejudices and passions of the hour,

misunderstood his motives, assailed his statesmanship,
and condemned his management of the great questions he was called to solve, now largely admit he
was misjudged, and concede to him the credit to
which he is entitled. Even our brethren of the
South, notwithstanding the animosities of war, are
disposed to recognize his claim to the respect, admi-
ration, and gratitude of the country.

In looking through his character we find most conspicuous his pure and lofty patriotism. He loved his
country with all his heart and soul and mind. We
can believe him when he said, standing in the hall
whence the Declaration of Independence was issued,
"I never had a feeling, politically, that did not spring
from the sentiments embodied in that instrument. If
the country cannot be saved upon its principles, I
would rather be assassinated on the spot." All he
said and did, both before and after he reached the
Presidency, showed that he kept the political truths
and the political principles embodied in the sublime
Declaration constantly before him as his inspiration
and guide. He was, without doubt, ambitious; but
his ambition was of a generous and lofty character,
ever subordinated to the single desire to serve his
country and advance its best interests. He did not
seek to raise himself to power by subverting the laws
and trampling on the rights of the people, like so

many recorded by history in her most mournful pages; nor did he resemble him so graphically described by Lucan as rejoicing to have made his way by ruin, —

" Gaudet viam fecisse ruinâ."

He looked for advancement from the gratitude of the nation, and sought the fame of the patriot who is solicitous for the common good, and devoted to the interests of the State. He wished not to destroy, but to preserve.

HIS INTELLECTUAL QUALITIES.

Mr. Lincoln's early life was a hard struggle against poverty. He had none of the advantages of early education, and few opportunities for mental culture until long after he reached manhood, for all his time and energies were occupied in getting a livelihood. He never acquired any great amount of learning. In respect to many subjects he may be said to have been very ignorant; but such was the force of his natural capacity, and the clear and logical character of his mind, that he may be placed in the ranks of those described by Tully, "who, without learning, by the almost divine instinct of their own mere nature, have been of their own accord, as it were, judicious and wise men; for nature, without learning, often

does more to lead men to credit and virtue, than learning when not assisted by a good natural capacity."

He read but few books, but it is evident that he
digested well what he read. He mastered principles,
and applied them to the subject under consideration
with exquisite accuracy. What he knew he knew
well and thoroughly. It could not be said that he
was learned in his profession, but he acquired the
reputation of being a sound and safe lawyer. As a
nisi prius lawyer he was very eminent, and few of
those who practised at the same bar with him had
greater power or more success with juries, whether
he attempted to convince or persuade.

A large share of his attention was given to the
study of politics and questions of government. His
public speeches and writings showed he had thought
long and deeply on these subjects, and comprehended
them so well that he was equally fitted for legislation
and administration. He was the Palinurus of the
ship of state, and through his good judgment, discre-
tion, and firmness, it was able to weather the dangers
which threatened its destruction. Like the Trojan
pilot, also, he was heedless of his own safety in the
discharge of his duty, and in the care of the trust
committed to his charge; and, alas! like him, too, he
was destined to sacrifice his life to the cause of his
country.

HIS MORAL QUALITIES.

His moral seems to have been more fully developed than his intellectual nature. All the accounts represent him as "kindly affectioned," tender-hearted, full of sweet and gentle charities, ever ready to sympathize with the heavy-laden and afflicted. His early struggles in life made him appreciate the sufferings of the poor, and he felt for them.

He was a plain, rough man, simple in his habits and ways, of incorruptible integrity, with a strong sense of justice and a conscientious regard for truth. It has been said, by those who knew him well, that he appreciated so fully the beauty of the right, and the deformity of the wrong, that, able and eloquent as he was as an advocate, he could not argue a case to the jury with his usual force when he felt he was on the wrong side. He could not be strong in the championship of a bad cause. He could not, like Belial,

> "Make the worse appear
> The better reason."

"On the right side of a case," said a competent critic, "he is an overwhelming giant; on the wrong side, his sense of justice and right makes him weak."

So well known was his character in these respects, that the people in his section of the country all knew

him and spoke of him as "Honest Old Abe." He
never corrupted his intellectual or moral nature,
either by doing wrong that good might come from
it, or by advocating error because it was popular;
and his statesmanship, always practical and straight-
forward, showed how unswervingly he followed what
was just and right.

There seems to have been no *vindictiveness* in his
nature. He was ever for mercy. His tenderness to
those who had endangered the safety of our armies,
by desertion and other military crimes, was almost
culpable. And it is owing to his forgiving nature
that there was no prosecution and punishment of
those who had made war upon the government.
When it was urged that the Nemesis demanded Jefferson Davis should atone for the terrible sufferings
he had brought upon the country, he replied, in the
sublimest strain of Christian charity, "Judge not,
lest ye be judged." On one occasion a friend was
denouncing his enemies. Lincoln said to him, "Hold
on; remember what St. Paul says: 'And now abideth
faith, hope, and charity. But the greatest of these
is charity.'" His love of justice is set forth with peculiar and pathetic tenderness in his reply to Douglas when they were stumping Illinois in 1858.

"Certainly," said he, "the negro is not our equal
in color; perhaps not in other respects; still, in the

right to put into his mouth the bread that his own hands have earned, he is the equal of every other man, white or black. All I ask for the negro is, that if you do not like him, let him alone. If God gave him but a little, that little let him enjoy." Can anything be more manly, honest, just, and charitable? If Lincoln read but few books, he certainly read his Bible, and kept in remembrance the Sermon on the Mount.

This gentleness and softness of heart did not make him weak. He was strong and inflexible when duty required him to be so. One of his intimate friends remarked of him that he "had the firmness, without the temper, of Jackson."

There seems to have been a strange vein of sadness underlying Mr. Lincoln's character, which affected his whole life and conduct. It was probably a constitutional dejection, rather than a grief resulting from disappointment or misfortune. This idiosyncrasy expressed itself in his homely face, for, despite the wit and humor in which he so often indulged, there was an ever-present pathos which no gayety could wholly repress. "His mirth," says his biographer, "was exuberant; it sparkled in jest, story, and anecdote, and the next moment those peculiar, sad, pathetic, melancholy eyes showed a man familiar with sorrow and acquainted with grief."

Mr. Lamon, the law-partner of Lincoln, says, "It would be difficult to recite all the causes of his melancholy disposition; that it was partly owing to physical causes there is no doubt; but his mind was filled with gloomy forebodings and strong apprehensions of impending evil, mingled with extravagant visions of personal grandeur and power. His imagination painted a scene just beyond the veil of the immediate future, gilded with glory, yet tarnished with blood. It was his destiny — splendid but dreadful, fascinating but terrible. He never doubted for a moment but he was formed for some 'great or miserable end.' He talked about it frequently, and sometimes calmly. He said the impression had grown upon him 'all his life.' The presentiment never deserted him; it was as clear, as perfect, as certain, as any image conveyed by the senses. He had entertained it so long that it was as much a part of his nature as the consciousness of identity. . . . He was to fall, and fall from a lofty place, and in the performance of a great work. The star under which he was born was at once brilliant and malignant."

The historians who shall hereafter portray the character of those who took prominent parts in our great civil war, like those who have given us the characters of the eminent men who have illustrated the annals of other nations, will paint, more or less, according to their political partialities and prejudices; but all, of whatever party or sect, who

> " nothing extenuate
> Nor set down aught in malice,"

must concede that Mr. Lincoln was a good and a great man; that his benevolence was large, his motives pure, his integrity unsullied, his ambition unselfish, his patriotism exalted, and that, by his prudence, sagacity, skill, and firmness, he saved the Union and preserved the republic which Washington founded.

He has gone to join the spirits of the just made perfect. He has entered the communion of the noble army of martyrs in the cause of country. He has been received into the fellowship of the illustrious of every age and nation.

No monument of granite or bronze is needed to perpetuate his memory, and hold his place in the affections of his countrymen. His fame will suffer nothing from the corrosion of time, but increase with the advancing years.

> *Crescit, occulto relut arbor ævo*
> *Fama Marcelli. Micat inter omnes*
> *Julium sidus, celut inter ignes*
> *Luna minores.*

www.ingramcontent.com/pod-product-compliance
Lightning Source LLC
Chambersburg PA
CBHW030009030726
47499CB00008B/2974